Double-Teamed: MMM First Time Football Romance

Van Cole

Published by Van Cole, 2022.

DOUBLE-TEAMED: MMM FIRST TIME FOOTBALL ROMANCE

First edition. December 7, 2022.

Copyright © 2022 Van Cole.

ISBN: 979-8223416166

Written by Van Cole.

Table of Contents

Double-Teamed
MMM Football Second Chance Romance

By: Van Cole

Foreword

There's nothing more difficult than keeping a secret in high school. Trust me, I'd know. That's actually one of the many reasons I decide not to attend my 10 year reunion. But, when I find out a very close friend from high school is attending, I figured, why not. We were just friends back then, but I always had a major crush on him. A part of keeping my secret meant I could never tell him that. So, we casually catch up at the reunion, about him playing for the NFL, and we end up at his hotel room where his boyfriend is staying. What follows is a passionate whirlwind of hot, male threesome action where all my high school dreams come true. But, what happens when morning comes, when the alcohol stops working? Was it just a one night stand or is there more to our story?

Double-Teamed

Chapter 1

Adam opened up his laptop, as he did every morning. He wanted to check his email before his sister arrived, as she told him she'd be in the neighborhood and wanted to drop by for a morning coffee. He liked it when she visited, but that happened less and less, because they were both busy with work and life in general. She recently got married, and they were planning on starting a family, so Adam cherished these peaceful moments with his sister, for as long as he could.

He scanned his emails quickly and disinterestedly, then saw one from a person he hadn't heard from in about 10 years. The subject of the email was just: Reunion.

Adam turned sickly pale. He looked at the calendar on his laptop. Has it really been 10 years? His brain was in a state of disbelief, but the facts didn't lie. Neither did the mirror.

He opened the email and started reading aloud, skipping every other word.

Dear Adam... cordially invited... 10 year high school reunion... would be a pleasure... everyone there....

But, he stopped before even reaching the end. He saw no point in it. He wouldn't be attending anyway. That was the end of it.

At that moment, he heard the doorbell, and closed his laptop. Ten minutes later, he and his sister were sitting comfortably in the kitchen, at his big ivory colored, dining table, next to the open window. Adam had recently moved to the outskirts of the city, and every morning, instead of the hustle and bustle of the city, he'd hear occasional chatter of passing people and birds chirping from the nearby park. It was quite a change, and one he loved.

"Anything new?" Stephanie was eyeing Adam from behind her coffee cup, taking a sip, then putting it back on the table, which separated them.

"Yeah," he nodded, with a mild lack of interest. "I got an invitation to go to our 10 year high school reunion."

"And?" she asked, expectantly.

"What do you mean? Of course I'm not going," he said, matter-of-factly.

"Why?" she seemed surprised.

"Are you seriously asking me that?" Adam frowned.

He already drank his coffee in one go, as he usually does. Plus, he was a little agitated now because of that email. He really didn't need that, especially now that things were going so well for him, both professionally and personally. His ex dumped him about 5 months ago, and Adam finally stopped moping about it, and continued with his life.

"I really don't understand," she shrugged her shoulders.

She was only 3 years younger than him, and sometimes, she acted like they were 10 years apart, or so it seemed to him.

"You know what a horrible experience high school was for me," Adam was still frowning.

"But, it's been 10 years," she urged him, "people change."

"Oh, do they now?"

He felt like he was snapping at her, but he didn't really want to. He just wanted to forget all about that email invite he got, and go about his business as usual. Not like there was anybody he wanted to see anyway. But, it seemed that his sister just wouldn't let this be.

"They won't stuff me into a locker this time. Probably cuz I don't fit in there anymore. Luckily," Adam continued, getting a horrifying glimpse of his high school days.

The teasing, the bullying, the name calling. The last thing he wanted was to relive any of that in any form. He was just glad when it was finished, and ever since then, he had absolutely no intention of going back ever again. He even went so far as to promise himself that. Now, Stephanie was being a smart ass, telling him how therapeutic it would be for him to go.

"Aren't you being a little dramatic, Adam?" she rolled her eyes at him.

"You were Miss Popularity. Everyone loved you. You're not allowed to speak."

He grabbed his cup, forgetting that it was empty, brought it to his lips and only then realized there was nothing to swallow. He frowned, then put the cup back on the table.

"I'm serious," he spoke more calmly. "You go there to see people, right? Well, there's no one I wanna see."

"Are you sure about that?" she tilted her head a little, asking this.

"What do you mean?"

"What about that guy you were best friends with?" she paused for a second, trying to remember his name. "You used to hang out with him like all the time."

"Blair Mathis?" Adam knew exactly who she meant. There was no else. There never was.

"Yeah, Blair!" Stephanie nodded. "What about him?"

"What about him?"

"Don't you wanna see him? Catch up? Have a drink?" she asked, and immediately noticed that the very mention of his name intrigued Adam.

But, Adam wasn't replying. He seemed lost in his own thoughts, miles away. He remembered Blair, his dark brown locks he never wanted to cut, his smart-guy comments when others would tease them. Adam never understood why kickers never got even half of the attention the quarterback or other players got. It didn't seem fair. Somehow, he was never one of the guys. Adam knew how that felt. It was the first thing that brought them together.

"Hey?" Stephanie waved her hand in front of him. "Earth to Adam?"

"What?" Adam snapped back to reality. "What did you say?"

"I asked why not see if he'll be coming."

"We... lost touch." Adam shrugged his shoulders, as if it was all out of his hands now.

"There is no such thing as lost touch in the 21st century," Stephanie extracted her smart phone out of her jean pocket and started typing. "Blair Mathis... let's see..." she waited a few seconds, then continued. "There we go! He plays for the NFL... Wolf Pack... has Facebook, Instagram, Twitter... Just send him a message and voila! Now, you can't say you lost touch."

She turned off her phone, placed it on the table and gave her brother a victorious look. She was a smartass and she knew it. They both knew it.

"We haven't spoken in years. I can't just pop out of the blue like that, hey, what's up, you going to the reunion?" Adam frowned again.

"Why not?" she asked, "do you need a special reason to reach out to someone you used to be BFF with a long time ago?"

"It's just... silly," he couldn't think of a better word.

"You're so outdated," Stephanie laughed. "It's like you're from the 50s or something."

Adam sighed. He knew she was right. He'd always been a little socially awkward, and even though he knew how to handle his phone and his laptop, he wasn't a big fan of social media in general. He preferred eye to eye conversations and having real friends with real dates and real coffees to drink. Sometimes, even he himself thought he was so old-fashioned, but there was nothing he could do about it. There was nothing he wanted to do about it, really.

Their conversation continued on a pleasant note, Stephanie updated him on some of the things she was doing, including her new colleague, who was apparently very handsome and very single. However, Adam wasn't really listening to what she was saying about this new guy, partly because he wasn't interested in a new fling and especially not in a new relationship, as the wounds from the old one were still too fresh. Also, he was too focused on the possibility of seeing Blair after all this time.

Chapter 2

Adam was looking at a Facebook page on his laptop. The name before him was Blair Mathis. Since they weren't friends, Adam could see only some info about him, and no photos. But, he had enough to go on, if he wanted to. At first, he thought of sending him just a basic message, but immediately changed his mind.

"It's stupid, isn't it?" Adam eyed his cat lounging comfortably on the sofa.

Orpheus opened his eyes, as if he knew that Adam was talking to him. His tail flicked to and from for a second, as if he was about to do something, but then it slumped back around his behind, and Orpheus' eyes were closed once more.

"Some help you are."

Adam adjusted his reading glasses, as if that gesture would reveal which course of action he should take. But, nothing happened. He was stuck in a limbo, and for a second, felt like that nerdy kid from high school again. A cluster of goosebumps ran up and down his back, as if the mere memory of that time made his entire body shiver with disapproval and a silly fear that it might happen again if he went to that reunion.

Then, he checked Google, and lo and behold, there were many photos of Blair Mathis for the world to see. Adam's finger scrolled fast, eager to see the change in his former friend's appearance. To his surprise, Blair seemed to have change very little. His brown curls were darker now, but still there, untouched by time and scissors, and the dimples in his cheeks still had that devilishly boyish charm. Adam assumed Blair probably had it made with the ladies. Not that this came as a surprise. Girls were all over him, even back in high school. Yet, Blair was always too picky, always finding some fault with any girl that practically offered herself on a platter to him. Adam didn't understand this, but he had no objections to his best friend spending the evening hanging out with him, instead of some girl. Adam himself kept shooting down offers from girls, but he had a different reason for that.

Then suddenly, he heard his phone ring. He reached out and grabbed it, but the number displayed wasn't any he recognized. He figured it was probably someone from work, as that was usually the case with unknown numbers.

"Hello?" he replied in a casual, but businesslike tone.

"Hi, is this Adam Thompson?" a female voice asked.

"Yes?" Adam replied, not really sure if he was replying or asking another question.

"Oh, hi!" the voice chirped another greeting, "this is Stella. Stella Rowen?" she added quickly, seeing that just her name didn't really ring a bell.

"Stella!" Adam replied quickly, remembering her as the girl who always organized all their gatherings in high school. Apparently, this position was still hers. "How are you?"

"I'm good, thanks. Just got back from vacation, and my kids were being little rascals. I swear, this is the last time I'm taking them. Next time, it's mom time! Oh, don't mind me. I always say this, then I change my mind, hahaha!" she kept on yapping, as she usually did.

Adam realized that his sister was wrong. Probably nothing's changed that much, even after 10 years. People rarely change the core of their character, unless something life-altering happened.

"Oh, but silly me! That's not why I'm calling," she continued to Adam's slight annoyance, "I'm actually calling everyone who didn't reply to my email about the reunion."

"Yeah, about that..." Adam scratched his head. "I was gonna reply, but..."

"You have no idea how many people told me that!"

"I can imagine," Adam rolled his eyes, but then remembered what Stella was like in high school. If she was still anything like that, he shouldn't be annoyed by her. He should feel sorry and be understanding.

"Only about ten people RSVP'd," she told him.

"Oh?" Adam raised his eyebrows. He figured this was his way to find out if that special someone would be attending. "Do you think you could tell me who those people are?"

"Why sure!" she jumped at the opportunity to talk about what she was doing, and obviously yearned for praise of a job well done. "Lemme just get my list... here... ahem... Jamie Mitchell, Ben Wells, Alana Espinoza, Charlie Collier, Blair Mathis, Beverly Hardy, Kayden Palmer, Ryleigh Chan, Lennox Barnes and Jada Turner," she finished her list all proud, waiting for Adam to comment.

The truth was, Adam was listening intently only until the fifth name. Then, Stella's voice trailed off into oblivion, and all Adam could think about was confirming his arrival.

"So, that's all the people," Stella added, expectantly.

"I see," Adam nodded.

"And, because the rest of you people didn't reply to my email, I have to go about it the old fashioned way," she scolded him in a playful way, so Adam didn't mind.

"You're really a doll for doing this. All of this," Adam wanted to stroke her ego a little, seeing she really needed it.

"Why, thank you!" Stella chirped from the other end of the line, more than happy to hear that. "Finally someone who appreciates all I do!"

"I really do," Adam continued nodding, more to Orpheus than to her really. "And, I'm real sorry I didn't reply. I just got caught up in work," he said the first thing on his mind.

"I know," she added. "That's why I figured there was no point in sending a follow up email, but go straight for the phone!" she giggled.

"Right you are," Adam replied, "so, lemme just RSVP right now."

"So, you're coming?" she asked, her tone of voice revealing that there was more to it than just mere reunion.

It was then that Adam remembered - all those whispers between Stella and her friends when he'd pass them by, her awkward smiles and hello's in the hallway, and the anonymous love notes he'd be getting, decorated with hearts about him and this other person, and how they belonged together but that it could never be. He still had them, all of them. The notes, the pressed flowers in between, everything nestled neatly in a little box, in his wardrobe. He never really knew who the notes were from, but something always told him it was Stella. Of course, he could never reciprocate her feeling because... Well, there were so many reasons, which he wasn't able to tell her about back them.

"Adam, are you there?" she whispered into the receiver, almost as if she was whispering in his ears, after a long session of love making.

"Yes, yes, of course," he replied quickly, realizing that he got lost in his own thoughts. "I'm coming. Sign me up."

"That's wonderful," she giggled, and he remembered the high school hallways once again. "I'm... so happy I'll get to see you."

"I'm happy, too," he replied, a little clumsily, realizing that if they prolong this conversation any more, it might transgress into a touchy area, one Adam wasn't willing to go back to. "Stella, I'm really glad you called," he started, hoping to end it quickly, "but I'm in the middle of something now, and I really have to go back to it."

"Oh, of course..."

He heard disappointment in her voice, but it was not his place to comfort her.

"See you at the reunion then," he continued.

"Of course," she repeated, her voice now automatic and lacking that cheerfulness she had in the beginning.

"Bye Stella!"

Adam hung up the phone, without even waiting for her to say goodbye. It was already becoming a little unpleasant. He remembered how Blair used to make fun of Stella liking him so much, and how it was obvious to everyone but Adam. He was simply oblivious to people and things which didn't concern him. Unfortunately for her, Stella was one of those people back in high school, and she was still one of those people now.

Chapter 3

"How do I look?"

Adam walked out of his bedroom and into the living room, where his sister was sitting comfortably on the sofa, petting Orpheus, whose eyes lazily opened, hearing the sound of Adam's voice.

"Look at you!" Stephanie whistled, impressed with what she was seeing. "I don't think you made such an effort to look good like.. ever!"

"Not funny," he frowned, jokingly. "I'm serious."

"So, am I," she nodded, "just look at you."

Adam walked over to the big, elongated mirror in the corner of the living room. He loved it. It used to belong to their late grandmother. A few weeks after she died, Stephanie and he went to her house. Their mother said she couldn't join them, because it was just too painful, so the brother and sister, hand in hand, walked into the house which once brought them so much laughter and happiness as children, but which was now so huge and empty. Adam got the mirror and some of his old toys. Stephanie wanted the vanity table, where she, her mother and her grandmother used to spend afternoons together, putting on make up and trying out perfumes. The rest was left intact, and eventually their mother found the courage to go back. Now, years later, she was happily living there, that house becoming her home once again.

Adam looked at his own reflection in the mirror. He had a haircut the previous week, so his hair was still formed as he wanted it to be, and some styling products never hurt either when one wanted to look extra nice. He freshly shaved this morning and did all the necessary grooming. It took him about two hours, but he didn't mind. It was Saturday, a day he could spend any way he wanted.

He always preferred the less is more approach, especially in his attire. His style was always understated, but classic and impeccable. A crisp white shirt and a black bow tie, with burgundy polka dots, and of course, plain black pants to boot.

"Maybe I should have dressed more casually. I don't even know what kind of an event it's going to be," Adam wondered aloud if he was overdressed for the occasion.

"Does it matter?"

His sister was making a good point. He shouldn't be dressing for others. He should dress to make himself feel like a million bucks. And, he really was feeling that way. In polka dots.

"You're right," he smiled.

"Of course," she grinned. "So, how do you feel?"

"A little nervous," he admitted, adjusting his bow tie more out of a need to do something while talking.

"About Blair?"

"Mhm," he nodded, gazing at himself in the mirror, "he's the only reason I'm going."

"Is he coming alone?"

"No idea," he shrugged his shoulders.

"I read that he isn't married, no kids, no girlfriend."

"That doesn't mean anything," he replied, "you know these guys sometimes like to keep their private lives ...well, private."

"But, something would still leak to the press. And, nothing has, so far," Stephanie added, "so, he's good at hiding either because he really appreciates his privacy ...or?" she eyed him mysteriously.

"Or?" he repeated.

"He has something to hide."

"Don't be ridiculous!" Adam burst out laughing. "What could he have to hide?"

"You never know," she shrugged his shoulders.

"You know," he told her lovingly, "I envy your imagination. You always think someone is either a murderer or a mysterious lover, there is no in between for you."

They both laughed. Over the course of the years, Stephanie's love for the written word really kept amusing him, especially when they were little kids, and she would invent stories to keep him entertained. With her, everything was a possible clue, anyone a possible suspect for a wrongdoing. Sometimes, he'd forget how lucky he was to have such a fun loving sister, who always stood by his side, no matter what. Not everyone was so lucky.

Chapter 4

The reunion took place at a cozy little restaurant, which was closed to the public for the purposes. Adam parked his car a little down the street, then slowly walked over to the restaurant. He stopped in front of the entrance, and glanced through the glass door. The place seemed packed. People were sitting at specially decorated tables. It looked like everyone was having fun. He even recognized a few faces. Then, he took a deep breath, adjusted his polka dot bow tie just a little, and took a bold step inside, pushing the glass door open like a cowboy in the Wild West. He couldn't help but feel a sense of being an outcast, even after all these years. It was a feeling that would probably never go away.

The hostess was sitting at her desk, right at the entrance. She smiled a row of pearly whites, framed by a fiery red lipstick. Her eyes revealed a cheerful person, of about Adam's age, and her voice completely suited her sunny persona. She was definitely gorgeous, by any standards, and that was probably the reason why she got this job in the first place, as her smile was warm and welcoming.

"Hi there," she beamed, "here for the reunion?"

She looked down at a piece of paper which had some writing, but Adam couldn't distinguish what it was.

"Yeah," Adam confirmed, nodding slightly.

"And you are?"

"Adam Thompson," he responded, waiting.

"There you are," she found his name easily on the list, then put a mark next to it, "feel free to go in. Almost everyone is here already."

He looked towards the place. It really looked like he was among the last ones to arrive. But, that was always a better option than arriving first.

"Is there like a seating arrangement or something?" he wondered.

"No, feel free to sit wherever you want. The menus are on the table, and when you're ready to order, someone will be with you shortly," she informed him sweetly.

"Thanks," Adam nodded once again, for good measure, then went in with a wobbly step.

He heard about this restaurant a while ago, from a few friends who all recommended its good food and pleasant ambiance. Adam had to agree. The place was cozy, and very inviting. Almost like a good friend opened up a restaurant at his place, and just kept inviting people to come in. The interior design was a combination of several styles, rustic, modern, a few vintage items were lying around, too. At first glance, it somehow seemed wrong, as if none of those things agreed with each other. But, on second glance, harmony would set in. The music would align with the feel of the vision, and somehow, everything would fall into its rightful place. At least, that was the impression Adam got.

He kept looking around, trying to find the least occupied table. Just as he thought, people were still separated into the same cliques as back in high school. Jocks were still sitting with jocks, cheerleaders with cheerleaders, nerds... there were only a few of them. Adam was surprised to see even that many of them came. He was still scanning the room for the least conspicuous position, which would allow him anonymity, unless he himself wanted a bit of the limelight. But, that was a rare occasion.

"Adam!"

Suddenly, Adam heard his name being called out. He froze in the same spot he was standing, cursing his luck. All he wanted to do was slither into the darkest corners of this restaurant, and here he was, being called out by name in front of everyone.

"Over here! Adam!" the voice repeated, a little too eagerly for his taste.

That someone was persistent. For a second, Adam thought of sitting down anywhere, and just pretend that he hadn't heard Stella call out to him. But, before he could do anything, he already felt a cold hand on his elbow, tugging at him.

"You came! Come, sit with me."

Without waiting for him to reply, she pulled him, and in less than a second, he was sitting at a table, surrounded by Stella and her weird friends from high school. He recognized all of them. They waved at him enthusiastically, and he just smiled back awkwardly, at what they giggled nervously, throwing serious glances at Stella, whose puffy cheeks were glowing red. It was like they were all back in high school.

Adam felt uncomfortable. His palms were getting clammy, and that bow tie was a little too tight. Nothing felt right. He didn't make the entrance he was hoping for, which was a silent and invisible one. Instead, he was sure that everyone noticed him. He wanted to just sit down and scan the room for any familiar faces which he liked, or at least, used to like. Now, he felt like all those prying eyes were already on him, devouring him with their unwanted curiosity, and all he could do was hope that Blair was late.

"The salmon is very good," Adam heard Stella speak into his ear, a little too close for his taste, showing him the menu.

"Really?" he replied, clumsily, "I'll have to check out the menu then, but I'm not really hungry honestly."

He reached out, and as he did so, he forced Stella to move to the side a little, leaving his personal space uncontaminated. He hoped it would remain like that, at least for a while. He opened the menu and pretended to be reading it, because that gave him a reason not to look in her direction or talk to her.

"Oh, I think this wine is really getting to me," she kept on talking.

Adam didn't want to be rude to her. After all, she didn't do anything to him. But, she was becoming increasingly annoying, and he was frantically scanning the room for any other person he could use an an excuse to leave her side. It really was like back in high school. Stella was nice and all, but he wanted her as far away from him as possible, because she could be too much sometimes.

At that moment, he saw him. Blair Mathis. Mr Irresistible. Mr Perfect Curls. Mr Everything. He was looking straight at Adam.

Unapologetic. Hot as Hell. Eyes fixated on him beckoning him to come. Then, he raised his hand just a little, barely visible, for one second, only to fold his elongated fingers and place that very same hand down, back on the table.

"Excuse me, Stella," Adam spoke to her, without even looking at her, "I'll be right back."

He didn't care whether she would get upset or not. He got up, making sure not to make any sounds with his chair, not even giving her a chance to say anything, and he walked over to Blair's table, with Stella's eyes watching his every move like a hawk. He could almost feel her gaze burning a hole in the back of his head, but he couldn't care less about that right now. He was mesmerized, called forward by an invisible force to come and take what he came for... if he had the guts.

He stopped in front of him. The table was in the corner of the room, so the lamp lights barely shone on it, leaving it mysteriously in the dark, and Adam could see only the left, illuminated side of his face. There was a trace of a faint smile, and those dimples girls were ready to die for back in high school. Blair was sitting opposite him. To his left were two young men Adam recognized as Blair's ex team mates. Now, they looked more like businessmen than athletes. And, it seemed like Blair wasn't all that interested in talking to them. Besides, they were too busy catching up and paid no attention to anyone else. Adam was just fine with that.

Blair didn't take his eyes off of him. His head tilted slightly to the side, as if wondering what Adam's next move would be. Adam felt like he was teasing him to do something, calling him out, so he didn't think. He just acted.

"Hey, Blair, long time no see," Adam walked over as confidently as he could, and sat down on the empty chair next to Blair.

Blair waited a second, even raised his eyebrow, as if he was surprised by this bold step.

"You, too man," Blair replied finally, with a hint of a mysterious smile.

Adam wasn't sure, but for a second he thought Blair had checked him out, and not in a friendly way either, but in a way a wolf checks out his prey to see if the meat was tender enough. But, he immediately pushed that thought away. He was just overwhelmed by seeing Blair after all this time, and he was just reading into things a little too much. He hoped it'd pass before he made a fool of himself.

"Something to drink?" Blair asked, seeing there was no glass in front of Adam.

"Oh, yeah," Adam smiled, "I haven't ordered yet. I just arrived."

"I saw," Blair nodded,and Adam swallowed heavily. "I also saw that Stella stuck her claws into you deep."

"Stella?" Adam turned around, and then saw that Stella was still sitting at the same place where he left, saying he'd be right back.

She was staring at him, her look a mixture of sadness and annoyance. Adam waved nervously, then quickly turned around.

"I forgot to reply to her email, and she called me," Adam explained, "almost forcing me to come."

"Well, I for one am glad to see you here," Blair flashed a row of pearly whites, "let's drink to that."

He raised his hand and politely called for the waiter.

"I'll have another scotch on the rocks. My friend here will have..." he waited for Adam to make up his mind.

"Oh, I'll just have a beer."

"A beer?" Blair laughed. "What are we, back in high school? Have a man's drink."

"I don't really drink..."

"You should," Blair confided, "it makes life more fun."

Adam grinned nervously. He figured Blair must have already had a few shots himself. He was never so... open. Adam didn't know what to make of all this. Ten years was a long time and maybe some of them did change, hopefully for the better.

"You know what?" Blair shuffled in his chair, "scratch that scotch. Get us two snake bites."

"Right away," the waiter rushed and a minute later, came back with two yellow looking drinks, served in a shot glass, decorated with a slice of lemon.

"Is this tequila?" Adam looked at the shot glasses, then Blair.

"Nope," Blair grinned. "It's a man's drink."

He took one of the glasses and pushed the other one to Adam, spilling only a little on the table.

"It's Canadian whiskey with just a dash of lime juice. Bitter, but worth it," he raised his glass, and Adam immediately did the same. "Bottoms up!"

Blair downed it in a second, and Adam did the same, coughing a little once he was done. Blair laughed.

"Manly, right?"

"Mhm," Adam could only nod, wiping his mouth a little.

Throughout the rest of the night, drinks just kept coming, but Adam could barely remember ordering any of those. He stayed at Blair's table, and at one point, he realized that they were sitting there alone. Others seemed to mingle, or dance, or sit at the bar and chat. Everyone was actually having a great time, including Adam, leading him to the happy conclusion that he was glad he came, despite his initial animosity towards this whole idea.

"So, you got a family?" Blair asked, among other things.

"No, no one. You?" Adam quickly asked back, really curious about his old friend and his new habits.

"There's someone I've been seeing," Blair admitted, "but we're very open about our relationship."

"Well, you were always the ladies' man," Adam smiled, not surprised that his friend wasn't single.

"Yeah..." Blair replied, with a facial expression Adam couldn't read. "You know, I'm kinda done with this place. You wanna get outta here?"

"You mean, go, with you?" Adam asked, clumsily, cursing his own nerves.

"Yeah," Blair laughed.

"Sure!"

Adam was already up, grabbing his jacket. But, as soon as he did so, he felt someone's warm breath a little too close on his neck.

"Going so soon?" Stella asked him, eyeing Adam, then Blair, then Adam again.

"Yeah, we had fun, thanks for organizing this, Stella," Blair replied instead of Adam.

"Oh..." Stella didn't know what to say, so she went in for an awkward hug with both of them, clinging a little too long and too tight on Adam.

Outside, in front of the restaurant, Blair got his key from the valet, and led Adam to his fancy, new car.

"Where are we going?" Adam asked, before getting into the car.

"What?" Blair grinned. "Afraid I'll take advantage of you?"

"No, just... asking," Adam replied, laughing.

This was the side of Blair he didn't remember. Blair was always a little nerdy, clumsy even, but that didn't take away from his charm. Actually, it only added to it. But now, he seemed to transform into a full blown self-confident person who knew exactly what he wanted and he wasn't afraid to go after it. Adam only wished he reached that point in his life. He felt he was the same shy, nerdy kid from high school, and that had already kept him from going after some important things he desired.

"We can hang out at my hotel room," Blair suggested, "if you don't mind my partner being there."

"Sure, no problem," Adam got in, and they headed straight for Blair's hotel.

Adam really didn't mind the fact that Blair's girlfriend would be there. He figured, he'd have another drink or two, catch up a little more, then call it a night. He was already imagining Blair's girlfriend. Tall, probably long blonde hair, maybe Scandinavian pale to contrast his dark features, with a perfect body and perfect face. That's how Adam always imagined the lucky girl who got to end up with Blair. Simply gorgeous. Smart to boot. Blair wouldn't compromise on that.

They continued talking about unimportant things, but every once in a while, Adam noticed that Blair was becoming more and more playful, his jokes having a double meaning, and he even touched Adam playfully on the shoulder, elbow and knee a few times,making Adam's body feel a surge of electricity. If he hadn't known Blair from before, he could have sworn that Blair was flirting with him, and shamelessly so. But, he knew it couldn't mean anything. They just had a few too many, and Blair was just being overly friendly. There was nothing more to it, and it would probably all be forgotten the following morning.

When they got into Blair's room, there was a guy there, watching TV. He turned when he heard them come in, and walked over to them. As he did that, Adam couldn't help checking him out. He was definitely as good looking as Blair, but he didn't have that je ne sais quoi. His hair was short and slick, and his face was perfectly symmetrical, almost to the point where it was relaxing to watch him. He was freshly shaven, Adam could see that much, when the guy approached Blair, and gave him a peck on the lips, his palm resting for one just one brief second on Blair's face, then he moved away.

Adam could have sworn that nothing in the world would have shocked him more than what he just witnessed. And, it probably showed on his face, because Blair and his partner looked at each other, then burst out laughing. Adam watched them suspiciously, praying to God that this wasn't one of those hidden camera shows, where they revealed it was all a cruel prank on someone.

"Adam," Blair stopped laughing, but there was still a smile on his face, "this is Logan. My partner."

"Nice to finally meet you," Logan approached him with light steps, and shook Adam's hand, though not very vigorously, as if he wasn't used to such masculine first greetings.

"Finally?" Adam repeated.

"He still doesn't get it," Blair grinned at Logan. "Gotta love 'im."

"I'm sorry, I... I don't know what's going on here," Adam admitted feeling uneasy, and he was on the verge of walking right out of there.

"No, I'm sorry," Blair approached him, placing his hand gently on Adam's shoulder, "I probably should have told you something a long time ago, but I didn't have the balls."

"What are you talking about?" Adam looked at Blair, then at Logan.

"I think this isn't the time for talking," Blair approached him with slow, deliberate steps.

Adam swallowed heavily. He realized he shouldn't have drunk so much, especially since he wasn't the one to handle too much alcohol. Yet somehow, his senses were sharpened to the point where he could almost hear Blair's breathing, he could hear his body swooshing through the air to get to him, in this sexually charged up room. A second later, and Blair was standing right in front of him.

"I wanted to do this since that first time I saw you in the cafeteria," Blair whispered.

Adam could feel the warmth of his breath on his face. His whole body tingled, aroused by what was happening, and the methodical, left side of his brain seemed to be out for the night, leaving him only with the deepest desires of his heart. Adam felt like his very soul was stripped bare, for Blair to see, and somehow, he didn't mind. The cards were finally all on the table.

"You were wearing a blue t-shirt, with brown pants. You had a few books next to you on the table, as if you didn't want to lose them," Blair kept whispering into Adam's face, and Adam could almost feel the bitter taste of those shots they had earlier.

But, before Adam could say anything to that, Blair kissed him with a passion Adam had never felt before. No kiss would ever compare to this one, the intensity, the long cherished, secret desire, the explosion that was about to happen. Their tongues acted as if they had been always together, and now apart only for a while, but had found each other again in this incredible, unexpected whirlwind of passion. Blair's hand flew back to Adam's neck, guiding his head, sucking out the very air out of Adam's lungs. Then, just as suddenly as he grabbed him, he let him go. Adam opened his mouth, taking a loud breath. Blair smiled.

He took him by the hand, then led him to the bed. Logan was sitting there, on the edge of the bed, legs spread out. Adam smiled to the fact that he was barefoot. Blair walked Adam over and let him stand between Logan's legs, as if he was caged by these two men, and there was no going back. But, that was the last thing Adam wanted right now. It was as if all of his worries flew out the window, and all that was left was that throbbing sensation inside his pants, begging to be let out to play. Logan's fingers trailed the bulge inside Adam's pants, as Blair hugged Adam from behind, using his hands to unbutton his shirt, one button at a time. As he did so, Adam felt Blair's warm breath on the side of his neck, then the tip of his tongue playing with his earlobe. He groaned loudly.

Logan's hands moved a little upward now, finding Adam's belt and unbuckling it. Then, his trouser pants button, the zipper, and Adam's cock almost jumped out of his underpants.

"Someone's eager to play," Logan grinned.

"Do you want this?" Adam heard Blair's voice in his ear. It sent shivers down his spine.

"Mhm," he only managed to mutter, when he felt Logan's hands and fingers on his dick, playing with it.

"Then, just relax and enjoy yourself..."

With those words, Adam felt Logan's lips on his hardened cock. His mouth was warm and welcoming, he could almost feel Logan's saliva dripping all around his cock and down onto the floor. Logan took his sweet time, licking and playing, using his hands, his fingers, his lips, his tongue. He took it all in, and Adam could feel the back of Logan's throat. He shivered. His muscles tensed. It was too soon, he had to slow down.

As if reading his mind, Blair sat down on the bed, next to Logan who moved away from Adam to give Blair a gentle kiss, and then Adam could see them both go back to him, mouths wide open. Their tongues traveled all over his cock from both sides, as it stood erect between them, like a pillar. Blair took it all in, and Logan went lower, sucking Adam's balls.

Adam closed his eyes, his hips naturally leaning forward, to make them do it harder, faster, stronger. He felt his arms jump into the air, his head leaning backwards, allowing him to take the deepest breath of his life, as these two men offered the soft, supple warmth of their mouths to him. They sucked him, licked him, kissed and bit, constantly changing the intensity, allowing him to only reach the point of no return, but not go over it yet.

Then, they stopped, and Adam looked down, wondering what happened. Logan and Blair got up, gesturing at Adam to lie down on the bed. They joined him immediately after taking off their clothes. Adam was again in the middle, Blair coming to his left and Logan to his right. Blair pulled Adam towards him, with passionate kisses and groping. Adam felt Logan's hands on his behind, Logan's finger trailing the soft line between his cock and his anus. It tickled at first, and made him smile. Blair chuckled.

"Does it feel good?" Blair asked, their lips still pressed onto each other.

Instead of a reply, Adam kissed him even more hungrily, biting down on Blair's lip, as he felt Logan's finger press softly on the sensitive flesh which he was so eager to open up for them. Blair pulled him up again and laid him on his knees.

"It'll feel even better now," Blair whispered, standing in front of Adam, with his cock hanging out.

Adam spread his knees a little further apart, wanting, yearning, his mouth open to take Blair in. His lips clasped against Blair's cock, thick and long, it was even more glorious than Adam had imagined it. He choked on it, sucking on it, then took it all the way in, until his mouth was full and couldn't even open up anymore. But, he wanted it all.

Then, he felt the cold sensation of wetness on his asshole, and Logan's fingers spreading it all around. The pressure was imminent, always a little painful at first. But, he knew what to do. They all knew what to do. Adam kept sucking Blair off, as Logan slowly entered him from behind, pushing in just a little deeper, then taking a break for Adam to stretch out enough, to take more of him in, until finally Logan was all inside, pushing in all the way, then pulling out quickly, leaving a gaping hole which begged to be filled again and again.

Logan kept pounding his ass, his other hand jerking Adam off, slowly then quickly, changing the intensity, only to finally heat up the tempo, mercilessly fucking him, like it was the last thing he would ever get to do, so he wanted to do it for as long as he could and finish with a huge explosion. Just as Logan finished inside of him, Blair sprayed into Adam's mouth, the sticky gooey cum dripping down the corner of Adam's mouth, until he swallowed it all.

The three bodies slumped down onto the bed, sweaty and sticky, breathing as if they had just run a half-marathon. Adam felt divine, and totally happy, but he saw Blair turning his ass to him, as an offering, as they were lying on the side. Adam bit him on the shoulder, and Logan oiled Blair up, just as he did Adam. He was still hard as a rock, as he pressed the tip of his cock against Blair's asshole, which opened up like a flower only a little at first, then more and more. Blair dug his hands into the pillow, moaning. It was like music to Adam's ears. He wanted to ram into him straight away, but he knew he couldn't do that. He went in slowly, carefully, as Logan spread Blair's asscheeks for a better view.

Adam was going crazy. Never, in his wildest dream, did he think this could ever happen. Yet, here he was, fucking the guy he had the biggest crush on back in high school. He entered him completely, all of his cock buried deep inside of him. He danced with his hips, forward and backward, holding Blair by the hipbone. He had no idea anymore who was moaning, but it didn't mind.

"Yeah, fuck me, deeper..." Blair groaned.

It didn't take him long before he finally exploded into Blair's soft, reddened core.

Adam had no idea what time it was, or who fell asleep first. His body was weightless, sleeping in this room which still burned at the touch.

Chapter 5

The following morning, when Adam opened his eyes, it was still dark in the room. For a second, he had no idea where he was, and then he remembered. Two beautiful naked bodies were sleeping soundly next to him, on the huge, king-sized bed. Silence reigned in the room. Adam reached for his phone and saw that it was a little after 7 am.

He removed the limp arm which was covering his bare stomach, and slowly got out of bed. He tiptoed to the other end of the room, where his clothes from last night still lay scattered around carelessly. He put them on, making sure not to make a single sound. He had no idea why, but he had a gut feeling that nothing good could come of this, and he would only end up getting hurt. He'd been hurt so many times, he just wasn't ready for another heartache. Seeing this was Blair, Adam knew this would hit him like a ton of bricks. He knew he wouldn't survive such a heartbreak.

So, he finished putting on his socks, grabbed his shoes and crept out of the room, closing it with a click, which locked it from the inside, leaving the two bodies still slumbering, safe and sound. He stepped into his shoes, then went down the stairs. He hailed a cab, and in less than half an hour, he was unlocking the door to his home. He threw the keys into the little bowl, then threw his body onto the couch and buried his face in his hands, taking a deep breath. When he removed them, he smiled broadly. If it was a mistake, it was a damn good one, he told himself.

He tried not to dwell too much on what happened. He was shocked, sure. But, that explained a lot about Blair's behavior back then. If only he'd known back then what he knew now, things could have been so much different. But, there was no point in dwelling on maybe's. He got what he always wanted: Blair. Even if it was for only one night. Now, it was time to get back to real life. That was the only way not to get hurt, to simply get away and just leave this as a sweet memory.

A few days passed, and there were no words from Blair. Adam knew this was probably what would happen, but he still checked his phone a little too eagerly every time he heard he got a message. Then, about 3 days later, his phone rang. He checked it. It was an unknown number, and he knew who it was. Stella. He sighed once deeply, before answering.

"Hello?" he replied bleakly.

"Hey, Adam?"

The voice that asked for him wasn't Stella. Adam would recognize that voice in a million of others, all shouting at the same time.

"Blair... hey," he was now confused, happy, shocked and surprised, all wrapped up in one.

"I'm real sorry I didn't call sooner," he started with a sincere apology, "we had crazy long sessions, the coach is really on our asses. Just ask Logan. I haven't spoken to him either. But at least, you were nice enough not to grill my ass for it," Adam knew that Blair was smiling as he spoke. There was a slight difference in his voice when he did that, and Adam loved it.

"Oh, it's fine, no worries," Adam tried to sound as nonchalant as possible.

"Thanks for understanding, I really appreciate that," Blair said, "listen, why don't you come watch the game on Saturday with Logan?"

"Watch the game?" Adam just stupidly repeated the question, feeling caught totally off guard by it, as he already convinced himself that it would be best to just leave this whole thing alone and not continue playing, because someone was bound to get hurt. But, deep down, he knew that wasn't what he truly wanted to do, not now that he was so close to making his wildest dreams come true.

"Yeah," Blair insisted, "I've got tickets and special seats for my boys."

My boys. Those words would get stuck in Adam's mind, and they wouldn't leave him alone. He would go back to those two words every time he'd think of ending it out of some stupid fear of uncertainty, fear of love, fear of life itself. It was like he was punishing himself sometimes, and now, it was finally enough. He wanted to be happy with someone. Why couldn't that someone be Blair and Logan?

"Wow..." It was like Adam's brain wasn't functioning, and he could barely say anything.

"What do you say?" Blair asked, all hopeful.

"That... sounds great," Adam thought about saying no, for one billionth part of a second, but then said exactly what he wanted to say, not caring whether or not he would come to regret it.

This thing with Blair and Logan had made him so happy, happier than he'd been in a while, and he was reluctant to let it slip his hands so easily.

"Awesome!" Blair exclaimed, "I'll arrange it with Logan to pick you up and then I'll see you guys Saturday!"

"Great! Can't wait!"

But, Blair had already hung up, and Adam bit his lip for sounding too eager. That wasn't part of the plan. Actually, his whole plan went haywire the moment Blair called.

Chapter 6

Logan picked him up at the designated time, and they arrived to the stadium quickly. It was packed, as usual. Adam used to follow football before, when he had more free time and of course, in high school mostly because of Blair, but lately he wasn't really all that into it. He simply didn't have the time at this point in life, and usually, none of his friends or current boyfriends would join him, so going alone wasn't all that exciting. This was, however, a special occasion.

Adam and Logan got to their seats, and the game started shortly afterwards. Logan was a fiery supporter of the Wolf Pack, which was the team Blair played for. He was even wearing their black and purple jersey. Adam secretly wished for one. They followed the game closely, cheered Blair on, and he noticed them sitting there, waving quickly one time, when he was able to.

During the break, Adam realized that Logan was a really nice guy in general. He was incredibly good looking, in a different way from Blair though, but good-looking nonetheless. This usually made people think he was stuck up, full of himself and all around, not a good choice of company. But, Logan was actually intelligent, kind and very thoughtful, all of which surprised Adam, leading him to the conclusion that he also almost succumbed to the usual stereotype which he was trying to get away from himself.

When the game was over, the trio ended up at Blair's place. This was the first time Adam was there, while Logan already made himself at home. It was a nice and cozy place, one of those man caves the rich and famous usually have. Adam was surprised that everything inside seemed to be revolving around the idea of the masculine, with very little feminine added. The paintings screamed ferocious and wild, the colors were dark, with occasional splashes of orange, as if Blair took all the colors from the jungle and copied them into the interior design of his home. It was strange, but at the same time Adam felt like he could be himself here, with both of them.

"How about we order a pizza?" Logan suggested, opening Blair's fridge and seeing it was half empty.

"Great idea," Blair approached him from behind and smacked him soundly on the butt.

"Ouch!" Logan shouted playfully, "what the Hell?"

"I don't like to fuck on a full stomach, you know this," Blair grabbed Logan by the balls, but Adam could see it was all play. "So, we're gonna do it before we order the pizza."

"Fine by me," Logan bit Blair's lip, which made Blair tighten the grip around Logan's balls a little more.

"Fuck..." Logan hissed through clenched teeth.

"Yes, let's..." Blair grinned, his other hand gesturing at Adam to come over.

Adam did as he was instructed, mesmerized with this sexy game that was unfolding right before his eyes. He walked over the to marble, kitchen counter, and Blair pushed them both against it, his hands now resting hard on both dicks. Adam's mind didn't know whether to focus on the icy coldness of the marble he was leaning onto, or the scorching hot hand that had his balls in its grip.

"Now, I'm trying to figure out, which of you I'm going to fuck..." he eyed them both hungrily.

He licked his lips, as if he was already imagining the stuff that he was going to do to them. He finally let go of Logan and turned Adam with one easy motion of his arms as if Adam weighed nothing more than a couple of feathers, making him bend over the kitchen counter. Blair pressed the side of Adam's face onto the cool marble. He then pulled down Adam's pants in one swoosh. There was no please or thank you, it was so much different from that first time, and Adam felt a pang of excitement. He loved it hard and rough, he loved it when it hurt.

Blair pushed Adam's feet as far away as they could go, revealing his already hard cock, and his asshole.

"Sit down between his legs," Blair ordered Logan, who immediately slumped down there, his face on the perfect level with Adam's cock.

"You know what to do," Blair told Logan, and the voice with which he was issuing orders, made both men harder than ever. Adam was afraid he'd cum just by listening to Blair talk.

"I won't be gentle," Blair hissed into Adam's ear, his hand grabbing Adam by the throat, "so you need to know our safe word. It's jungle. If I'm too hard or you want to stop for whatever reason, just say jungle. Do you understand?"

"Mhm..." Adam nodded.

"I didn't hear that!" Blair growled, biting into Adam's neck. He was sure it'd leave marks, but right now, that was the last thing he cared about.

"Yes! Yes... sir..." Adam finally understood what was asked of him, and he was more than happy to oblige.

"That's better," Blair slapped him on the butt hard, leaving a burning red imprint of his hand on Adam's butt. But, Adam didn't flinch. He welcomed the stinging sensation, and prayed for more to come. "I might reward you now," Blair told him.

Adam didn't turn around. He heard the drawer open, then some noise as if Blair was trying to find something among other things, then the drawer was closed again with a slam. Then, the same cold, slimy sensation, and the warmth of Blair's fingers on his ass. As soon as Blair pressed against Adam's opening, Logan opened up his mouth and encircled it around Adam's cock, jerking himself off. He spilled some saliva onto it, his fingers spreading it all over, then his tongue played with the tip, up and down. Adam had no idea what was happening. His skin was on fire, hot to the touch, biting his lip, as Blair pushed himself inside more and more, spreading Adam's asscheeks apart for a better view.

"You feel so good..." Blair whispered into Adam's ear, but he barely heard it.

His brain was buzzing, as Logan was sucking him off hard and fast, and Blair was pounding his ass from behind. It was just too much. His body shook uncontrollably, his muscles hardened, as he tried to dig into the hard surface of the kitchen counter with his fingers, but instead only slid alongside it with his nails. He shot a full load of hot cum into Logan's mouth, and a few seconds later, Blair's nails dug into the soft spot on Adam's skin.

"Fuck, it's good...." Blair fucked him hard, harder than he ever fucked anyone before, wanting to be fully inside, every inch of him, and to fill him to the brim with steaming hot cum, which would then slowly drip out of his asshole.

A few more seconds, and it was all finished. The three men breathed heavily, sedated by a sudden rush of adrenaline, their minds and bodies in a blissful state. Silently, with gleaming smiles on their faces, they took a shower together, then ordered a pizza and watched a movie. Adam felt like this was what a perfect evening was supposed to look like, and he never wanted it to end.

Chapter 7

When Adam opened his eyes in the morning, he realized that there were only two naked bodies in the bed, one being his own. Logan was gone. Adam lifted his head a little. The room was dark, but the curtains allowed thin strips of sunlight to pierce through, so the room almost resembled a pagan temple of some jungle tribe.

He got up, ready to start getting dressed. He walked over to the dark, oak desk in the corner, because his shirt was neatly resting on the chair next to it. Then, he saw a little piece of paper. He knew he shouldn't, but curiosity got the best of him. He was glad he read it.

Had a lot of fun, guys. Have a great day! XOXO, L.

He smiled, putting the paper down. He tried not to make too much noise.

"You thinking of sneaking out again?"

Adam heard a still drowsy voice coming from the bed. He glanced over, and saw Blair propped up on a pillow, staring him down. His dark tresses fell over his eyes, but Blair didn't bother to move them.

"Yeah," Adam laughed nervously, raking his fingers through his hair.

"Why?" Blair cocked his head.

"I don't know," Adam walked over and sat on the edge of the bed, "I guess I'm just wondering what all this is."

"Are labels that important to you?"

"No, just... is this going anywhere? This..." he gestured with his hands at nothing in particular, "whatever this is."

"We're having fun," Blair continued, "isn't that enough?"

"I'm not really looking for just fun, you know me better than that," Adam spoke, then chewed on his cuticle, for which he got a playful slap from Blair. "Ouch!"

"I thought you quit that nasty habit."

"I go back to it only when I'm stressed out."

"Are you stressed out now?"

"I would just like to know where we stand," Adam admitted.

"Fair enough," Blair agreed, "listen, I wouldn't have gone through all this fuss to get to you if I wanted just fun. You know that, right?"

Adam nodded silently. Blair was definitely hot enough to get any guy, or girl for that matter, he wanted. He didn't have to come up with elaborate schemes for one night stands. He just needed to get down to the club and be himself.

"Good," Blair agreed, "because, if we wanted just a fling, we could get anyone at the club."

Adam believed him. Blair seemed to be reading his mind, it was crazy.

"But, you asking me to make some kind of promises..." Blair paused, "I'm not sure I can make any. Not right now. There's too much going on, and I need to sort some things out first. Something work related."

"I understand."

"For now, we could just see where it goes," Blair announced, "no pressure."

"I just don't want to get my heart broken," Adam admitted again.

"None of us do, trust me," Blair propped himself even more up, so he was now closer to Adam, and his hand rested gently on Adam's back, petting him.

"Alright," Adam nodded, but he wasn't convinced.

Still, this was a conversation all three of them should have together. Talking to just Blair about their possible future together and leaving Logan out, seemed a little unfair. So, Adam decided to leave it at that, and follow Blair's advice. He'd just see where it goes, and hope that at the end of this, he wouldn't be trying to mend the pieces of his broken heart.

Chapter 8

The following few days passed by uneventfully. Adam didn't really hear from Blair or from Logan, but he wasn't expecting to. Blair made it clear that he couldn't commit, at least not now, and Adam respected his decision. This would be a casual thing, and Adam decided he was OK with it. He was never the one to get too clingy, he expected the same from his partners. However, as soon as he starts to feel something more, he knew that would eventually be his cue to leave, unless everybody raised the stakes. But, that would be a bridge he'd cross when he got to it. There was no point planning a future which might never happen.

Work was unburdened, as Adam didn't get any new cases, and besides, his partner was more than happy to defend cheating husbands in court. Adam tried to be a correct lawyer - as much as that could be done, but that way, he got less cases, as he hated defending liars and cheats.

That afternoon, he was sitting at his office, just doing some paperwork, when his phone rang. It was a number he didn't have saved in his contacts, but he recognized the last 3 digits. For a second, he actually considered not picking up. After all, he was at work. But, he was a good guy throughout, and knew he'd feel bad afterwards.

"Hello?" he replied, knowing whose voice he'd be hearing.

"Adam, hi!" Stella chirped like a choir of sick mice.

"Hi, Stella," he replied, only half focused on the conversation, his other hand shuffling the papers before him.

"Is this a bad time?"

"Well, I'm at work, but I have a few seconds," he told her.

"Great! I um... I'm calling because I know you like football, I saw you last Saturday..."

He frowned. She was there? Was she spying on him? He immediately got paranoid. This was getting too weird, even for him.

"My dad is the Wolf Pack's number one sponsor, so we get all the stuff for free. Merchandise, tickets, everything really..." she kept on talking.

"Oh, that's nice," he said, not really knowing what he was expected to reply to this.

"I've been feeling a little down lately, ever since my ex left me and the kids, I don't really socialize with many people," she rambled on, "I guess the reason I'm calling is that I... um... I have two tickets for the game on Saturday, and was wondering if you'd like to go with me," she fired her invitation, and waited to see if it'd hit bull's eye.

Adam stopped scribbling on the piece of paper in front of him. A second was needed for her invitation to sink in, then he looked up out the window. The Wolf Pack was Blair's team. He hadn't really spoken to either Blair or Logan about plans for the weekend, but he was hoping they might hang out again. However, there was no word from either of them.

"Adam?"

"Yeah, I'm here, sorry," he quickly added, "just trying to remember if I had any plans for the weekend."

"Well, if you do..."

"I don't think so," he told her, feeling kind of sorry for her.

He thought he could just go to the game with her, and then, even if Logan's there, he could just get together with the guys after he said goodbye to Stella, keeping her at a safe distance. Something was telling him that Stella would keep on pushing, until he had to reveal to her the reason why he wasn't interested in her, and in all honesty, it had nothing to do with her personally. She was simply... a girl. That was enough. He'd make sure to let her down gently, and explain everything.

Adam never really hid his sexuality. He simply believed it was his own private matter, and no one was privy to it, unless Adam himself deemed them so. In other words, he wasn't flaunting it around, but he also wasn't hiding that fact. At least not like Blair did. That revelation came as such a shock, but for the first time ever, it was a shock which worked in Adam's favor. He checked online, and nowhere did it say that Blair was gay. On the contrary, his name kept popping up alongside some famous models, singers, rich girls, but never a guy. He wondered how Logan dealt with all that.

"Great!" she shouted so loudly from the other end of the line, that Adam thought she burst his eardrum, completely interrupting his stream of thought.

"I'll pick you up before the game. Just send me the address," Adam told her, completely indifferent to their little get together.

"Of course," she quickly added, "I'm so happy."

"I'm glad to hear that," he replied, trying to sound polite, but not give her false hope, "see ya Saturday."

He hung up immediately. He wasn't really sure how he felt about this, but he was hoping that this would give him the opportunity to get her off his back and focus on what was happening with Blair and Logan.

Chapter 9

At the game, Adam was only half present, his eyes constantly wandering around to see if Logan would be attending the game. Adam hoped he would. He already knew that Blair would be playing. That was a safe bet.

"Nice seats, right?" Stella tried to get comfortable, but her wide hips couldn't allow for that to happen completely. So, she shuffled a little, then stopped when it was least painful.

Stella was never what one would consider a beauty, but she had a certain charm. Unfortunately, time wasn't very kind to her, and she not only gained weight, but seemed to round up completely, resembling a fluffy donut one would rather eat than fuck.

"Yeah," he nodded, glancing at her quickly, but then his gaze went back to scanning the other seats for a familiar face.

At that moment, a guy carrying two Cokes and two hotdogs tried to squeeze through, but it was impossible, and he ended up spilling both Cokes right into Stella's lap. She immediately jumped up, her face inflamed as she started shouting.

"What the fuck do you think you're doing!? You motherfucker! Look at me!! I'm all wet now because of you, you asswipe!!"

Adam was shocked. He didn't think he ever heard so many insults in one go from a woman, especially a woman like Stella.

"I'm really sorry, ma'am," the guy seemed really apologetic and Adam could see he was a good guy who just happened to be a little clumsy sometimes. Unfortunately for him, this was the wrong moment to be clumsy.

"It's fine," Adam realized he'd have to interfere, otherwise Stella would just continue shouting at the poor guy, because she was getting ready to fire another round of horrible insults, "are you OK?" he asked her, offering some wet wipes he had on him.

"Thanks," she tried to wipe her skirt a little, but the stain wouldn't go away, so she just threw the wet wipe carelessly onto the ground.

"That was ...quite an array of insults," he tried a joke.

"Oh, sorry about that," she transformed back into her old, goody two shoes self, as if this crazy, curse wielding maniac never happened, "sometimes, I can't control my anger. My therapist says to count to 10 when something like that happens, but I totally forget to count, hihi," she giggled a little, which sounded strange, coming from a woman in her late 20s.

"You definitely didn't count there," Adam added, a little uncomfortably.

Then, as if coming to save the day, Adam heard a familiar voice behind him.

"Adam!"

He turned around, and faced Logan. He was dressed casually as usual, but he was sticking out like a sore thumb, with his good looks and killer smile, hidden underneath his baseball cap. Adam thanked his lucky stars.

"I tried calling, actually we both did, but your phone kept sending me to voicemail," Logan said.

"Really?" Adam quickly grabbed his phone from his pocket, and realized it was turned off.

He tried powering it back on, but nothing happened. Only a black screen.

"Shit," Adam raised his gaze, "I think my phone died."

"Hi, I'm Stella," she suddenly interfered, offering her hand to Logan, who seemed confused to see her there.

"Yeah, hi. Logan," he shook her hand quickly, but the look on his face told Adam that something was up.

"You OK?" Adam asked him.

"Yeah, just... we'll talk to you later," Logan waved awkwardly, then disappeared somewhere in the crowd.

"Come, sit down," Stella pulled Adam down next to her, but her hand remained on his elbow, as if it was stuck there.

Adam felt that there was something Logan wasn't telling him. He noticed the strange look on Logan's face when Stella introduced herself. But, what did he have in common with Stella? Adam wondered.

At every touch down, Stella would shout ecstatically, like a true fan should. But, whenever the opposing team scored, she turned back into the cursing sailor. It was almost comical to watch. The whole thing was just painful, and Adam sneaked a few eager glances at his watch, to see how long this torture would last.

When it was finally finished, they walked over to the parking lot and he offered to take her back home, even though it was only 6pm. He was actually hoping to drop her off and then go home, and try and contact Blair or Logan from his laptop, to see if they would be up for a meet up. The night was still young, as they say.

"I was actually hoping we could go somewhere and have dinner," she blinked her eyelashes a little too hard, making it appear as if she had something stuck in her eye.

"Yeah, about that," he scratched the back of his head, "you saw that my phone died, and I have to see what my friend wanted," he told her, knowing it was a flimsy excuse but he sucked at lying, especially if he had to do it on the spot.

"But, I thought this was going to be a real date," she continued, like a deserted puppy.

"It was just friends, catching up, watching the game together," he explained, "I'm sorry if I gave you the wrong impression."

"Did I do anything?" she wondered, and Adam thought he saw the twinkle of a tear in her eye, which made him feel like the bad guy.

"No, you didn't do anything, really..."

"It's because I have kids, right?" she wouldn't allow him to say one word. "But, it's not my fault my ex left me to take care of them..."

"Stella, Stella..." Adam spoke calmly, his hands now resting on her shoulders. "It's nothing you did. I swear. I'm..."

"Seeing someone, right?" she interrupted him. "I knew it. I just knew it. I hoped you were single, but, of course, how could anyone as wonderful as you be single for a long time, or even a short time..." she kept on rambling, as she usually did.

"No, I'm not really seeing anyone," he told her, simply because there was no label on what was happening with Blair and Logan, so it was best to keep it out of the limelight. "It's something else. I'm..."

"Just not interested, right?" she interrupted him yet again, and Adam had to laugh, because it was so annoying, but she seemed so desperate that he just couldn't be upset with her. "That was my other suspicion. I know I'm not much to look at. I'm nothing to look at, really. But, I was hoping that maybe, you'd see past my physical appearance..."

"Stella..." his hands were still on her shoulders, and he had to shake her a little to stop her from talking forever like this. "It's not that either. I've known you for years. Sure, we haven't been the best of friends, but I know you're a good, kind-hearted person, and anyone would be lucky to have you," he told her, in an effort to be nice. "Now, what I was trying to tell was that I'm..."

"Did you really mean all that?" she interrupted him for the third time, and Adam was now on the verge of telling her to go to Hell, and just leave him alone. Sometimes, she was too much, and right now, he was too eager to go home and talk to either Blair or Logan.

"I did," he nodded, hoping that would end this conversation, and she'd finally get into his car.

"Then, I do have a chance with you?"

"Stella, I..."

"No, shhh..." she pressed her index finger onto his lips, and he instinctively took a step back. "Just let me be hopeful. Even if nothing happens, this hope is going to make me happy, at least for a little while."

He wanted to tell her that all of that wasn't really healthy, and that she should always accept the truth as it was, and not demand an alternative which suits her better, but he really wanted to get home and open that laptop. Besides, he was feeling increasingly sorry for her, so he figured, there couldn't be much more harm than it would have been now, if he had told her the truth.

"Well, if that would make you happy," he shrugged his shoulders, unlocking his car and opening the door.

"It would," she confirmed, with a blissful smile on her face.

For a brief second, she was almost beautiful. That's what happiness does to people. It makes them shine from within, and that was exactly what was happening to Stella at that moment. She went to the other side, and immediately got in the car.

Chapter 10

Adam, Blair and Logan were sitting at a cozy restaurant having dinner. It was early in the evening, so the place was packed, but nobody was paying any special attention to them, and they were all enjoying it. The trio didn't manage to get together on Saturday, as Blair was busy with try outs, but they did manage to go out on Sunday evening for a special dinner.

"This was a great idea," Blair told Adam.

"Well, it's my fault really that we couldn't arrange it sooner."

"Why?" Logan asked, "your phone died. How is that your fault?"

"I should have got a new one sooner?" Adam replied, asking at the same time, and the three men laughed. "In any case, here's to all three of us just hanging out."

He raised his glass of wine, and the other two men joined in. Significant glances were being exchanged, then all three took a sip of their red wine.

"This is a great vintage," Blair licked his lips a little, feeling the remnants of the wine. "Logan told me he saw you at the game with ...Stella?" he paused a little before he said her name.

"Yeah. Why?" Adam wondered, cutting his beefsteak into small pieces.

He was surprised to hear Blair start talking about her so suddenly. He had no idea why talking about her was important under these circumstances. She was the last person Adam wanted to talk about right now.

Blair looked at Logan, then back at Adam. There it was. That look again, the same one that Logan had when he saw them at the game.

"Is someone gonna tell me what's going on or do you guys enjoy to keep me in the dark til the very last moment?" Adam asked, with a smile on his face, hoping it was nothing he should be worried about.

"Well, I gave Stella your phone number," Blair told him, "when she called about the reunion. She asked for yours in specific."

"Where did you get my number?" Adam wondered.

"I know some of your clients, but that's besides the point now," Blair explained. "The thing about Stella is that you should be careful."

"Careful?" Adam had no idea what this conversation was about or where it was going. "Why?"

"You know she liked you back in high school, right?" Blair asked, while Logan was only listening to the whole thing.

"I suspected, yeah."

"She was always jealous of me, because you used to spend so much time with me."

"I didn't know that," Adam admitted.

"Well, she didn't tell me specifically, but you could tell something was off, and that was the only explanation."

"OK, so what does Stella's silly, high school crush have to do with us now?" Adam asked.

"I think she's still in love with you," Blair told him. "Actually, she might even think she loves you."

"I doubt she loves me, but yeah, I think she's a little infatuated," Adam revealed. "That much was obvious when I was about to drive her home on Saturday."

"I'm telling you, just be careful. You need to end it, before it even starts, otherwise we could all end up on her revenge list."

"Why?" Adam repeated.

"Shit, where do I start?" Blair glanced at Logan for support, and Logan covered Blair's hand resting on the table, with his. It was just a moment, but it was enough support to allow Blair to continue with what he knew. "I have a gut feeling that deep down, she still hates me. Because of you."

"Because of me?"

"Yes, because of our ...friendship, back in high school."

"Why do you care now?" Adam asked. "We're not in high school anymore."

"But, her dad is the main sponsor for the team," Blair told him what Adam remembered almost that very same moment. "He could get me transferred or off the team, if he wanted to. That is, if she wanted to."

Adam understood now why Blair was so reluctant to talk about any specifics regarding their relationship. Things seemed to make sense now that Blair revealed everything, and somehow, Adam knew that all this was true. Stella appeared so suddenly in his life, and yet, she was completely unwilling to let him go. The memory of their parking lot conversation now sent shivers down his spine.

"Tell him about the husband," Logan suddenly added, and Blair 's eyes shone with something resembling fear.

"The husband?" Adam repeated, "I thought he left her."

"In a way, he did," Blair continued. "He died."

"Died?" Adam kept repeating what he was hearing, unable to fully digest these news. "I wonder why she'd lie about that."

"Because he died under suspicious circumstances," Blair explained. "She and the kids were visiting some friends, when their house burned down. Her husband was in it. By the time the firemen were there, he already died of carbon monoxide poisoning. After the police report, some things just didn't add up. She was questioned by the police several times, especially seeing that he had life insurance payable to her in case of his death."

"Are you sure?"

"I mean, I know as much as anyone else reading the papers. But, you know as well as I do, where there's smoke, there's fire. Sorry about the pun," Blair smiled awkwardly. "They say she spent a month at a hospital, psychiatric ward, because she was apparently so distraught by the death of her husband. Some said she faked it, to get the extra pity vote."

Adam remembered Stella's transformation at the game. Mild and sweet Stella became the enraged green monster in a blink of an eye. Then, equally fast, she was back to her usual self.

"But, this is all hear-say," Adam waved his hand dismissively. "This could all be just a huge coincidence."

"Sure, but it doesn't hurt to be careful."

"Of course," Adam assured them both, "I was gonna end it after the game, but she wouldn't let me, until I agreed to some twisted version of how things are."

"Just end it," Blair urged him. "And make sure she knows it has nothing to do with me. If she finds out, she can and probably will make my life a living Hell, with some help from daddy dearest."

"OK, I'll end it. No worries," Adam nodded.

Chapter 11

A few days later, Adam was on the verge of considering to change his phone number, the one he'd had for years. The same one which would be so much hassle to change. But, he had no idea what else to do at this point. The previous day, Stella appeared at his place, ringing his doorbell as if that was the most usual thing in the world, and totally expected of her.

"What are you doing here?" he asked her, standing at the doorway, without the slightest intention of inviting her in.

"You haven't been returning my calls," she told him, standing there like a little school girl who knew she'd been caught doing something she wasn't supposed to do. Adam didn't find it endearing at all.

"I tried telling you at the parking lot, Stella. I tried telling you the same thing over the phone a few days ago, and I've repeated it in messages several times. I don't know how else to tell you that this..." he gestured around with his hands in empty air, "us... whatever you think is happening, isn't happening."

He knew he sounded a little rough, but he was way past his last patience point with her, and he knew that sometimes, you just had to be more assertive to get your point across. Stella needed to be told like this. There was simply no other way than to be the bad guy.

"We went out on a date, you can't deny the attraction that exists between us, Adam," she loved saying his name, that much was obvious from the way she worded it.

"There is no attraction," he corrected her.

He hated having this conversation in the hallway of his apartment complex, where any nosy neighbor can hear what's going on, but he was damned if he was going to let this woman into his home.

"You're wrong," she shook her head, "I know you. I know you better than you know yourself, and we belong together," she kept on talking, as if she was in a trance, and nothing Adam told her even reached her.

She just kept repeating the same thing over and over again, like a broken record, unable to listen to reason.

"Do you hear yourself?" Adam was in disbelief. "No, I'm done. Please leave me alone. Don't call me. Don't reach out. Please, Stella," he tried to be as kind to her as possible, but it was getting increasingly difficult.

"You don't know what you're saying," she kept shaking her head, with an almost psychotic smile on her face, "I'll give you some time, then we'll talk again."

"No, we won't talk ag..."

But, she wasn't listening to him. She had already turned around, and was walking down the stairs, her heels clicking and reverberating throughout the hallway, like a hollow reminder that this was far from over.

Adam closed his doors, and buried his face in his hands, in annoyance. Things were getting really out of hand, and if all those things Blair mentioned were true, then Stella really wasn't someone you should mess with.

A few days later, this encounter was still haunting him. Initially, he thought it would be easy to get rid of her. People usually understood when you told them no. He wondered if he should have told her about him being gay, but he then remembered what Blair told him earlier. If Stella found out about this, she'd connect the dots. She'd realize that something must be going on between the two men, and that might create problems for Blair. That was the last thing Adam wanted.

He cursed his luck for making this so complicated. All he ever wanted, ever since high school, was for Blair to like him in a romantic way, and for them to be together. Adam thought that wouldn't be possible, not in a million years. Now somehow, the Universe aligned so that Adam felt like the luckiest man alive, but of course, dreams can never be obtained without overcoming obstacles. Stella seemed to be a difficult and very persistent one.

That evening, a few days after his unpleasant talk with Stella took place, Adam was lounging on his sofa in the living room, reading his book, when he heard the doorbell. He glanced at his watch. It was past 8pm. He had no idea who it could be at this time. Stephanie usually called before dropping by, and he hadn't spoken to either Blair or Logan since the day before yesterday. Adam wanted to tell Blair about his chat with Stella, and Logan happened to be there, so they all discussed it shortly, not wishing to dwell too much on something that unpleasant. All they could hope for was that she wouldn't make good on her threat.

He sighed, dropping his book onto the cushions, then got up to open the door, neglecting to look through the keyhole. As soon as he opened the door, the sight surprised him.

"What are you guys doing here?" he smiled, immediately moving to the side to let Blair and Logan inside.

"We figured you might need a little cheering up after that God awful episode with that loonie," Logan raised his right hand to reveal a bottle of wine.

"You read my mind," Adam grinned locking the door.

"You OK?" Blair approached him and gently caressed his cheek.

"I am now," Adam replied, "and she's the last thing I want to talk about right now."

He went to the kitchen, and brought three glasses, putting them on the little coffee table in the middle of the room.

"Did we interrupt your pleasant evening at home?" Logan picked up Adam's book.

"No, not really..."

"We promise to make it better," Blair grinned, biting his lip, looking at Adam.

As the two stood facing each other, Adam felt Logan's presence behind him. Logan's hands first rested lightly on his hips, then those same fingers dug deeper into his skin, through thin pajamas. Adam got hard instantly. Blair's lips found his, his tongue exploring hungrily, as if they all hadn't seen each other in months. Logan's hand traveled down, into Adam's pajamas, finding his thick cock throbbing with excitement.

"Happy to see us, I see..." Logan whispered into Adam's ear, biting on his earlobe, and Adam felt a million little goosebumps travel up then back down his body.

Blair moved a little backwards, and as if on cue, Logan pulled down Adam's pants from behind, pulling down his boxer shorts, too at the same time. Blair licked his lips a little, then got down on his knees before them both. Logan's hand traveled up to Adam's neck, grabbing him by the throat forcefully, pressing on it, but still allowing Adam enough air.

"Fuck..." Adam groaned, as he felt Blair's warm breath on his cock.

Then, the juicy inside of his mouth. Blair played with his tip first, licking it, showering it with a million little, butterfly kisses, as if it was a temple that should be worshipped. Then, he swallowed it in one go. He moved away, spat on it a little, watching the saliva drip downwards, stretchy and gooey, like cum. But, not yet. Blair took him all in again, the tip now hitting hard against the back of his throat, as he played with Adam's balls with his other hand.

Logan's hand kept squeezing around Adam's neck, then releasing his grip only enough to allow Adam one big gulp of air, then squeezing again, feeling Adam's quickened pulse on his fingertips.

Adam was resting his head backwards, on Logan's shoulder, his hands grabbing a handful of Blair's curly locks, as Blair's head moved forward and backward, first at a slow pace, then faster and faster, until Adam couldn't hold it anymore, and he came into Blair's mouth in one big gush. He could feel Blair's tongue playing with the sensitive tip, as it was still dripping inside his mouth, and the motion of his tongue when he swallowed the whole load. Blair opened his mouth, releasing the grip he had on Adam's still erect, throbbing cock, all wet and shiny.

"Fuck..." Adam repeated.

"You already said that," Logan whispered into his ear, and the men laughed.

"We're not done yet," Blair got up, wiping the corner of his mouth with his fingertip sensually, and Adam was already looking forward to what would happen next.

But, a loud banging on the door interrupted them.

"You expecting anyone?" Blair asked.

"Just be quiet and they'll go away, whoever it is" Logan said silently. He didn't really want to stop playing their game.

"I don't know who that is..." Adam quickly pulled up his boxer shorts and his pants, then walked over to the door.

He looked through the keyhole, and jumped back in fright, because he saw a huge eye gazing back at him.

"What happened?" Blair asked from behind.

"Shit, I think it's her..." Adam raked his fingers through his hair, in an effort to calm himself down.

"Stella?" Logan whispered, and the two men nodded.

"Just be quiet, I'll try to get rid of her," Adam urged them, clearing his throat a little.

He opened the door only enough for half of his body to show through. On the inside, he placed his foot behind the door, so she couldn't catch him off guard and push it open.

"Stella," he tried a smile, barely managing to pull one off.

"Hi, Adam," she replied.

She seemed dressed for a special night out, with her shimmery dress which hugged her curves in all the wrong places. Her make up was aggressive and he couldn't stop looking at her lips and the weird way she put lipstick even over the lipline.

"You like what you see?" she asked him, protruding her left hip a little, and he realized that he was looking at her a little too long, but this only gave her the wrong impression, and that was the last thing he wanted right now.

"I came to take you out," she told him, as if he expected her to.

"Out where?" he asked the wrong question.

"Anywhere you want, really," she shrugged her shoulders, taking it as a certain yes.

"Stella…" he sighed heavily, "how long do you plan on keeping this up?"

He was still trying to be the good guy and let her down gently.

"Silly, until I get what I want, of course," she purred.

"And, what do you want?"

"Isn't it obvious?" she took a step closer to him and the door, and Adam instinctively pressed his foot down even harder, the one that was guarding the door. "You."

"Seriously, Stella… do I have to be horrible to you so you'd leave me alone?" he shook his head.

He really felt sorry for her. She definitely looked like she had some unresolved issues, but he doubted she did any of those things Blair accused her of. She didn't have it in her, and Adam still didn't want to hurt her feelings, out of some weird sense of loyalty for outcast friends from high school.

"But, why are you acting this way?" her voice trembled.

"Because I don't like you that way. We can be friends, but nothing more," he told her, for the millionth time.

"It's Blair, isn't it?" she suddenly said, her nostrils flaring.

"No…" Adam immediately replied, "what makes you think he has anything to do with this?"

"He kept us apart back in high school, but don't let him keep us apart now," she begged, her voice down to a whisper.

"Stella… no one kept us apart back then, and no one is keeping us apart now," he assured her, on the verge of just telling her he was gay so they could end this.

But, he also knew that if he told her that, a whole new shitstorm was about to take place, and Blair would be in the epicentre of it.

"It never had anything to do with Blair or you," Adam could hear himself raising his voice, but he really couldn't remain patient anymore.

"It's always been me. I was never attracted to you and I never will be. No matter how many times you come to my door, how many messages you leave, how many of those love notes you left me back in high school..."

But, at that moment, there was a look of surprise on her face, as if he had told her something she didn't expect.

"I sent you those love notes."

Both Stella and Adam turned back to look into the room, as Blair stood behind Adam, and was now in plain sight before both of them, despite the door being only ajar.

"It was you?" Adam couldn't believe what he was hearing.

"Yes," Blair nodded, "and I can't sit by and allow you to take all the blame for what was happening. Stella told me she liked you back in high school. She wanted me to talk to you about her, to see if you liked her back. I..." he paused, "I lied to her that you had a girlfriend from some other school, so you weren't single. The truth was, I wanted you all to myself, but I had no idea what to do, how to talk to you. Hell, back then, I couldn't even explain who I was to myself, let alone to someone else."

Adam and Stella listened intently to this newfound knowledge. Adam had no idea, and he always thought those silly heart messages from his secret admirer were really from Stella. Now, it turned out it had been Blair all along, and he didn't figure it out.

"I knew it was you all along..." Stella hissed through clenched teeth of her now half-eaten lipstick. "You kept him from me back then, but you won't keep him from me now," she screamed as she tried to push the door open and attack Blair, but luckily, Adam still had his foot firmly planted behind the door, and she couldn't do anything.

Instead, she took a step back, her eyes flaring with malice and hatred.

"I'm giving you two days to leave Adam," she told Blair, "if you don't, you will be kicked off the team. No one else will take you in. I will make sure of that."

And with those threats still lingering in the air like a bad smell, she stormed down the stairs, leaving the three frightened men behind her.

A few minutes after Stella had left, they were unable to say a word. Each of them had a similar dark vision of their future together, and neither of them liked it. Logan stood in the corner, leaning sadly against the wall, where he was stationed a few seconds ago, with a completely different outlook on life. Blair was in the middle of the living room, his hands raking through his perfect hair, as his face showed signs of stress and fatigue. Adam felt like he was frozen in time and space.

"We can't let her get away with this," Logan said first, seeing he was the one with the least to lose.

Adam was walking up and down the room, with Orpheus' eyes watching him closely, as he had no idea the kind of stress his master was under. But, then again, he didn't really care.

"We won't," Blair assured them. "I'm the only one responsible for the choices in my life, and I'll be damned if some loonie is going to force me to do something or not."

He was almost growling, his tone of voice bordering on shouting. Adam knew how he was feeling. His life was about to crumble down, unless he did what someone told him to do. Something he didn't want to do.

"You know what she can do," Adam told him calmly, remembering who her father was.

"Yeah, she can ruin my life."

"Maybe... it's just best we leave things as they are, and not see one another again," Adam suddenly added, defeated.

That would be the easiest option, from a certain perspective. They just end things right now, they each go through a little heartache, and everyone eventually goes their own way. It all sounded simple enough, but such things always sounded so simple in theory, while practice was a whole different ball game.

"Do you really mean that?" Blair asked, truly surprised by what he had just heard. "Tell me honestly. Because, if that's how you really feel, then there's no point in discussing anything further."

He sounded upset, hurt, surprised. Adam knew why he'd feel this way, but he was just offering an option which might be the best, under the circumstances.

"You know I don't," Adam replied immediately, without thinking.

He didn't really need to think about that answer. He knew exactly how he felt about Blair, how he felt about Logan, and also, how he felt about their relationship. For the first time in a long time, he was happy, but truly happy, with the kind of happiness that didn't come from a superficial feeling of contentment, but actually a sensation of one's heart being full. Deep down, he was already imagining white picket fences and the three of them living together, somewhere where they could all be happy. But, he knew that was just a dream. Still, a man could hope.

"Then, why are you even suggesting it?" Blair continued, a little angrily, "instead of trying to come up with a solution."

"There is no solution," Logan finally said what they were probably all thinking.

"No, this bitch isn't going to dictate who I get to fuck or be with," Blair was fuming at this point. "If she does something, I'll talk to the coach. He'll believe me."

He ended on such a note that it was obvious that Blair was done talking about it, so Adam decided to let it go, at least for now. From this perspective, it really looked hopeless, and Adam hoped a good night's rest would help them find a way out of this mess.

As it was expected, none of them was really in the mood for any hot action after this, so instead, they decided to watch a movie, and went with a classic such as Cruel Intentions. Adam had always loved that movie, but this time, he simply couldn't focus. He kept thinking about Stella and how she had come into his life, threatening to tear it completely apart. Not only that, she would be destroying Blair's life, too, because once his football career was over, he knew Blair would never be happy again. Football was his life, it had been the only profession he's ever known. Without it, he would be lost. Adam knew that.

So, the only way was to make Stella see reason somehow. Talking to her seemed impossible. It was like talking to a three year old. She kept repeating what she wanted, and it was like she wasn't even listening to what someone else was telling her. Such a conversation was doomed to fail from the start.

At one point, Adam didn't even realize that he had dozed off. He opened his eyes, and saw Orpheus sleeping wrapped up around his legs. Adam was covered by a blanket he knew he kept in the bedroom. So, someone else must have covered him. But, there was no one there. The apartment was empty, only a little lamp in the corner shone bright, revealing a little note on the coffee table.

Adam reached for it. It read:

Don't worry, we'll figure this out. Love you. B&L

Adam smiled. He would have loved to believe what that note said. It would be so easy to do so. But, he knew reality was far more complicated than that.

He petted Orpheus, who stirred a little, giving him a little meow. His fur was soft and warm, and Adam wished he could be like Orpheus, too: a little fluffy darling, who only cared whether someone fed him and petted him, nothing else in the world mattered.

Chapter 12

A few days later, Adam was still feeling uneasy. This whole situation sounded like something out of a romance movie, but this time, he wasn't sure who would get their happily ever after, because it seemed that all the characters of this romance were doomed. Unable to focus on work, he still tried, sometimes successfully, sometimes not. He was sitting at his office, completely listless, his body mechanically signing those papers and replying emails, but his mind was miles away, far away from these problems which he had no idea how to solve.

"Mr Thompson?"

Adam heard a quick knock on the door, then it swung open only a little, revealing the frizzy haired head of his secretary.

"Yes, Linda?" he replied.

"There is a man here to see you. I told him that he needed an appointment, but he said it's urgent," she continued, uncertain if she did the right thing by interrupting him.

"What's his name?"

"Mr Holt," she paused to remember his name, "Logan Holt."

Adam immediately stopped and placed the pen on the table. He glanced at her.

"Send him in."

"Alright, Sir," she disappeared and instead of her, Logan's face appeared a second later.

He walked in, closing the door behind him. He seemed to have aged several years in the last few days. It was like he wasn't the same handsome man Adam met a few weeks ago.

"Logan, what's wrong?" Adam got up, giving him a hug.

When he wrapped his arms around Logan, it was like Logan had lost some weight, too.

"You look like shit," Adam told him, "no offense."

"None taken," Logan smiled weakly, "can I sit down?"

"Of course," Adam jumped before him, pulling the chair to help him sit down. "Something to drink?"

"No, no...", Logan waved his hand in a gesture of dismissal, "I won't be staying long."

"Did something happen?" Adam was beginning to get worried.

Logan didn't reply. At least, not immediately, but his silence said it all. Adam knew well what the reason could be.

"Is it... Blair?" Adam whispered.

"He went to practice on Monday," Logan started, with a deep and painful sigh, "the coach told him that he didn't need to come to practice anymore."

"Why?" Adam knew how stupid that question sounded, but he wanted to know if they at least offered a semi-plausible excuse as to why he was being kicked off the team.

"They told him he was being transferred."

"Transferred?"

"To Alaska.," Logan revealed.

Alaska. Adam didn't even know they had a football team.

"When?" Adam asked.

"They haven't told him yet, but he's guessing it's soon."

"Where is he?"

"Home. Moping. Drowning in his good buddy Jack."

"Shit..." Adam tensed his shoulders, "I can't let this happen. This is none of his fault, and he's taking the full blame for it."

"That's why I came here now, he doesn't know..." Logan continued, "I ... I know it's not your fault either, but could you talk to her? Maybe beat some sense into her?" he chuckled weakly, as if trying to cheer himself up as well.

They both knew he wasn't serious. It was just that both of them were out of options, seeing the man they loved beaten down.

"I can try. Talking some sense into her, I mean," Adam smiled bleakly.

It was highly unlikely that she'd change her mind just because Adam asked her to. But, it was at least something they could try.

"That's all I'm asking," Logan got up, "I.. don't know what to do... seeing him like that..."

"You love him, don't you?" Adam asked.

"Yes," Logan wiped a little stray tear, "so do you."

"Since day one," Adam admitted.

"We have to help him..."

"I know," Adam agreed.

He hugged Logan, then walked him out of his office. When he closed the door, he knew exactly what he needed to do.

Chapter 13

It was about 8pm when Adam drove up to Stella's place for the second time. The first time, he was just picking her up, but this time, he knew that he would be going in, no matter what. He tried preparing for this conversation, but no amount of mirror practice could even come close to him feeling ready for this.

He took a deep breath, standing there in front of the main gate, gathering up the courage to press that buzzard. A few seconds later, he finally managed to do it. He then turned to face the camera. There was no voice greeting him, just a buzzing sound signaling that the gate was open and he was invited in.

Adam drove up to the house, and parked his car a little down the pathway. As he walked, the gravel crunched beneath his shoes, and the door opened up before him, as he was walking up the shiny, marble stairs.

"What a pleasure!" Stella's voice chimed through the hallway as she spoke. "I didn't expect to see you."

"May I come in?" Adam asked, instead of a greeting.

"Of course," she moved away to let him pass.

She was wearing a burgundy, silk bathrobe, obviously not expecting any visitors at this time. Adam thought she might want to be excused to change into something more decent for company, but she showed no such inclination.

There was something different about her. There was no sweetness, no kindness. Her face was stern, even though there was a smile on it. What Adam felt was a bitter smell of victory won by trampling over others. She seemed to enjoy it. He wondered what happened to that sweet nerdy girl from high school, or was she always like this, he just didn't see it? He wasn't sure anymore. What he was sure of, though, was the fact that Blair had to stop paying the price for this shitstorm. If anyone would be paying, it would be Adam.

"I think you know why I'm here," Adam said, having walked into a long hallway which seemed to lead to a sitting room, but he wasn't planning on staying too long. Just to say what he needed to. For that, he could easily stand. Then, they'd see what would happen next.

"I do?" she asked, her eyes aglow with a wicked shine.

"I'd appreciate it if we didn't play any games. You know you won. Blair is being transferred."

"He is?" she asked again, but he could judge from the sound of her voice that she knew perfectly well what he was talking about. She was just playing.

"Of course, and it's all because of you."

"You can't say I didn't warn you," she gave an indifferent, half-shrug.

"That's the reason I'm here, to make you change your mind."

"What can you offer to make me change my mind?" she asked, a little too seductively.

"Myself," Adam said, his voice broken down to a whisper.

"What do you mean?"

"Don't lash out on Blair. It's not his fault. It's me you should be mad at," he paused a little, then continued, "stop the transfer, and I'll do whatever you want."

"Whatever I want, huh?" she eyed him like a piece of meat, and he felt uncomfortable to point where he wanted to cover up with something more than jeans and a shirt, maybe a thick fur coat.

"Yes. Just leave him out of this."

"You really think I'm stupid, don't you?"

"What?" he frowned, "no, no."

"I stop the transfer and you go behind my back, and get back together or something. No way."

"No such thing will happen. Football is Blair's life. Give it back to him and you can have me."

It was the most difficult thing he ever had to say. He knew that he loved Blair with all of his heart. He loved both men so much that he couldn't imagine his life without them in it. But, he also knew that Blair would be a broken man if he got transferred somewhere like Alaska. It was also questionable whether he'd be staying on there, or whether they would just keep transferring him until either they or him quit for good. Logan might follow him up to a certain point, but he might lose Logan, too, and he would be left with nothing he loves.

This way, it would be like the three of them never met that fateful night at the reunion. They would continue with their lives, and Adam would be paying the price for it. But, that's what love is. Sacrifice. Undying devotion. Full commitment. Doing everything in your power to make that other person happy. Adam wanted to make that sacrifice for Blair and Logan, because he loved them more than life itself.

"Prove it," she told him, suddenly.

"How?" Adam had no idea what kind of proof she was looking for.

"Make love to me, right now," she told him, undoing the belt of her silk bathrobe and letting it fall to the ground, revealing that she was wearing nothing underneath.

Adam wasn't expecting that. At least, not so soon, before he had any time to prepare for what he might be forced to do, so she could leave Blair alone.

"If you want me to take your offer seriously, you need to prove to me that you really mean it," she explained, taking one, bare step towards him, "and what better time than now?"

When she got close to him, he could smell lilies in the air, as if she had just taken a shower, using a lily scented shower gel. He forced himself to look at her, while deep down, all he wanted to do was shut his eyes and walk out of there blind as a bat. In all honesty, she didn't look that bad. She was constantly wearing unflattering clothes, so she appeared flabby and a little unkempt, but now he could see that her body was not that bad to look at. For a female body, that is. He tried to imagine Blair in front of him, because after all, he was the reason Adam was going through this torture. But, he couldn't.

"Take off your clothes," she instructed him, leaning in for a kiss so close that he could smell her strawberry lip balm, but she didn't kiss him.

She took a step back, as if to see him better undressing. He took off his shirt and threw it to the ground. He continued with his belt, then pants, letting them fall down, then walked slowly out. He was wearing only his boxer shorts now, but he felt like he was stripped down to his very soul, painfully exposed for the world to see.

"All of it," she gestured with her index finger, transforming into a ruthless, sex hungry fiend, which was something Adam never knew she could become.

He swallowed heavily, then took the sides of his boxer shorts with his fingers, and pulled them down quickly, like pulling off a bandaid. Now, he was wearing just his birthday suit.

"Now, come and kiss me," she told him.

He did as he was instructed. He walked over to her, lifeless, like a puppet whose arms and legs were broken and in pain. He stopped in front of her, and as he raised his hands towards her face, he brushed against her hardened nipples. He didn't feel anything. His cock was dangling listlessly, not realizing that it was time for action.

He leaned in, and pressed his lips against hers. She opened her mouth, wanting more, and he gave it to her. His tongue played around with hers, his hands pressing gently on the back of her neck, dictating the tempo.

All of a sudden, she moved away, wiping her lips with her fingers. She looked at him with an expression he couldn't figure out. But, he was getting pissed off. She was getting what she wanted. Why would she continued playing these games? Just to mess with him some more? Wasn't this enough already?

"You were really gonna do it, weren't you?" she asked.

Now, he really didn't understand what the Hell was going on here.

"Of course," he nodded, wondering why'd she'd ask him such a stupid question.

"Of course," she repeated, a little more silently, caressing his cheek as she did so. "You were always such a good man, Adam Thompson. No wonder you would do this for someone you love."

"What is all this, Stella?" he asked, covering himself with his hands, at least the parts that fit in them.

"I just wanted to see how far you'd go for him," she started explaining. "I just wanted someone to love me like you love Blair," her voice was breaking down, and she sounded like she was about to start crying any minute.

"So, this is all a game to you?" Adam felt like screaming at her for putting them all through this.

"No, I really like you, Adam. I always have. But, I think I just realized that, even if I did have you by my side, you would never be mine. Not really."

"Stella..." he started, feeling that this was again the Stella he had known and appreciated always.

"No, no, let me finish. In high school, I just thought you guys were best friends, and I thought I could be your third person, you know. But, you never needed that third person. At least, not me. I think I get it now."

"I never meant to hurt you, Stella, neither did Blair," Adam explained.

"I know, but I did hurt you."

"It's nothing that can't be fixed."

"I'll tell daddy to stop the transfer. I'm sorry about that. I was just blinded by what we could have, not realizing that you already had it with someone else, and it wasn't right for me to try and break you up."

She started sobbing, and Adam went to give her a hug.

"I have to admit, this is the weirdest hug I've ever give to anyone. Naked and crying," he told her, and they both burst out laughing.

"Yeah," she added, wiping her eyes, "let's get dressed."

Adam's head was still spinning from what just happened, but this just proved one important thing. The Universe did have a way of unfolding so that people could be happy together, even if it's in the strangest way possible.

Chapter 14

The following evening, Adam was resting on the sofa. Orpheus was nestled cozily next to him, on his special cushion. Adam tried to get ahold of Blair all day, but his phone was switched off. He also tried to call Logan a few times, but there was no reply, and it kept sending him to voicemail. He was sad that he didn't get to share what happened with Stella immediately, but he was hoping that there would be plenty of opportunity for that in the following days.

Suddenly, there was a knock on the door, disturbing the pleasant silence that reigned inside Adam's apartment. So many things had happened lately, that he was actually yearning for a peaceful evening with no distractions. However, it seemed someone else had different plans for him.

Drowsily, Adam opened the door to see Blair standing there.

"Logan's parking the car," Blair explained without even being asked, "I just wanted a few minutes alone with you."

"Sure, come in," Adam slid to the side, allowing Blair to come into the apartment, closing the door behind him.

"The coach called," Blair continued, intertwining his fingers together as he spoke, "he told me the transfer was off, and that I was staying. He said how happy everyone was because of it."

Adam couldn't help but smile. Stella really did make good on her promise. Her word really meant something, whether that was a threat or a promise.

"I know you had something to do with it," Blair approached him, his deep eyes piercing him down, through to his very soul.

Adam felt like the only person who could ever see him fully, through all the masks and pretensions, was Blair. Despite seeing the naked truth, he still loved him.

"It doesn't matter," Adam told him.

To him, it really wasn't important what he needed to do. He would have done it all gladly, for the sole reason to see Blair happy. Nothing else mattered.

"How can you say that?" Blair looked at him in disbelief. "That's all that matters."

"What do you mean?"

"Stella called me," Blair said, "she told me everything."

Adam looked down. He didn't want Blair to know everything, especially not the part where Adam was willing to do something he swore he would never again do. But, she beat him to it.

"I'm sorry, I..."

"Sorry about what?" Blair interrupted him with a smile. "For wanting to make sure I got what I wanted? For totally disregarding your own happiness for the sake of mine? Is that what you're sorry about?"

Adam smiled nervously, but all those feelings of uneasiness and shame and sorrow disappeared the moment Blair wrapped his arms around him and showered his face with kisses.

"Hey!" they both heard the door open and a familiar voice scolded them jokingly. "Why are you starting without me?"

The three men all laughed. It felt good to laugh again like this, knowing their troubles were finally over.

"I was just telling Adam how lucky we are to have him," Blair grinned.

"We sure are," Logan agreed.

"You guys..." Adam felt himself blush.

"So, we again thought you might need someone to celebrate your victory with," Logan revealed a bottle of wine in his hand once again.

"The wine magician has arrived!" Blair joked.

"Don't start with me," Logan threatened him, "otherwise we'll make you watch The Grey."

"What's that?" Blair asked.

"Is it that movie with Liam Neeson, about that plane that crashes in the wilderness, and the survivors are fighting a pack of wolves?" Adam asked, accepting the wine, then walking over to the kitchen to get the opener.

"Correction," Logan added, "the Alaskan wilderness."

Blair sent him a look of daggers, then all three men laughed again. As Blair and Logan got comfortable on the sofa next to Orpheus, Adam watched them from the kitchen. His house was full of joy and happiness, and finally, so was his heart.

*****

Don't miss out!

Visit the website below and you can sign up to receive emails whenever Van Cole publishes a new book. There's no charge and no obligation.

https://books2read.com/r/B-A-RTRV-TTCDC

BOOKS 2 READ

Connecting independent readers to independent writers.

Also by Van Cole

3 Man Huddle: MMM Best Friend Romance
His Alpha Wolf: Gay First Time Romance
A Dragon's Miracle: Gay Dragon MPREG Romance
Double-Teamed: MMM First Time Football Romance
His Football Star: Gay Second Chance Romance
Love In My Town: MM First Time Romance
Training A Hockey Star
Game Night
Double Shift
Take A Shot
Dear Professor
Getting Inked
Ninth Inning
Triple Threat
Seducing My Best Friend's Brother
My Protector
The Blueprint
Show Me The Way
End Zone
Matched To His Tiger
Love At First Puck
My Straight Boss
Falling For The Alpha
My Boss
On Thin Ice

www.ingramcontent.com/pod-product-compliance
Lightning Source LLC
Chambersburg PA
CBHW051251160726
47994CB00003B/1119